© Published by Pasty Peeps 2003

Reprinted 2004
Reprinted 2007

Printed by Rowe the Printers, (01736) 756435

PASTY PEEPS

CORNWALL

*Story and characters devised
by* Jools Hichens

Illustrated by Graham Hichens

In a pretty little cottage
in Cornwall, near the seaside town of
Hayle, lived the Pasty family.
Pixie Pasty, her younger brother Penrose
Pasty, Mummy Pasty and Daddy Pasty.

1

Pixie Pasty woke early one morning, peeped around her bedroom and saw the chink of bright light on her bedroom wall. She jumped out of bed, pulled back the curtains and let the sunshine pour into her room.

"Penrose ! Penrose !" Pixie cried.

"Summer is here, summer is here !"

Young Penrose ran into
Pixie's room and looked out of the
window. All he could see was clear
blue sky and bright yellow sunshine.

"Yippee ! Yippee !" Penrose cried, as
he ran around the bedroom.

"Come on you two !" said Daddy.
"Make your beds and
tidy your rooms,
after breakfast we are going to spend
the whole day at the beach and have
an ice cream on the way home."

Pixie and Penrose were very excited.

Pixie sorted through the toy cupboard
and found her red bucket and spade.
"I can't wait to paddle in the sea
again, and use my red bucket and spade
to build sand castles." said Pixie.

"I can't wait to hunt for treasure and look in all the rock pools for shells and things." said Penrose. "I'm going to put everything I collect into my favourite brown bag !"

Penrose always took his favourite brown bag with him wherever he went because he never knew what he may find, or what he may need !

The Pasty family left the cottage
together and walked down the
lane to the beach.

Pixie Pasty carried her red bucket
and spade,

Penrose Pasty carried his favourite
brown bag,

Mummy Pasty carried the beach towels
and
Daddy Pasty carried the picnic.

When they arrived at the beach they saw
that it was empty and quiet.

The sea was very, very big and blue
and it sparkled in the sunshine.

The yellow sand was warm and soft
under their feet.
Daddy Pasty noticed a huge rock on the
beach and thought it would be a jolly
good place to settle down.

"Come on !" said Pixie to Penrose. "Lets go and paddle in the sea."

"Be very careful not to wander too far away from us," said Mummy. "Or you will be lost."

"We'll remember !" said Pixie and Penrose together.

They ran down to the edge of the sea and splashed in the small white edged waves.

They paddled up and down, and down and up, splashing each other and having a great deal of fun, so much fun that they quite forgot what their Mummy had told them about wandering too far away !

It was quite sometime before Pixie
looked up and realised that
she couldn't see Mummy and Daddy Pasty
sitting on the beach anymore,
the beach had filled with people !
"Oh my goodness !" she said to herself.
"Penrose ! Penrose !" she called.
"We had better go and find Mummy and
Daddy or they will be very, very worried
about us, I think we may be lost !"

Pixie was right, they were lost !

14

Pixie and Penrose held hands
and were just about to leave
the edge of the sea when
they heard Mummy's
voice.

"Pixie !
Penrose !"
she called.
"It's time
to have our
picnic lunch."

Mummy pointed
to the very big rock.
Pixie and Penrose looked
to where Mummy was pointing
and saw their Daddy waving.

"Oh dear !" said Pixie. "We were having so much fun splashing and paddling we didn't notice how far away from you we had wandered."

"I know !" said Mummy. "But I could see you all of the time. You are the only little pasty on the beach with pink ribbons in your crust !"

"I'm ever so sorry Mummy." said Pixie tearfully. "And so am I." said Penrose.

Mummy smiled as she took hold of them by the hand and led them along the beach towards the rock and Daddy.

"Hello you two !" said Daddy. "I thought you were lost !" "We nearly were !" said Penrose. "Mummy found us !"

"We forgot to remember to never, ever wander too far away from our Mummy and Daddy !" said Pixie. "But I think we'll remember now !"

"I'm really hungry !" said Penrose.

"So am I !" said Daddy. "Lets eat !"

Mummy laid out a picnic of sandwiches,
cake and fruit. It was delicious.
All the splashing and paddling and
nearly being lost had made them very,
very hungry. Everything was eaten up.

Pixie and Penrose didn't wander far from their Mummy and Daddy again.

Penrose spent the afternoon collecting shells and other things which he put in his favourite brown bag.

Pixie played with her red bucket and spade building sand castles, whilst Mummy and Daddy read their books and enjoyed the sunshine. They all had a really wonderful time on the beach.

They were getting ready to make their way home when Daddy Pasty asked Pixie and Penrose what they had to remember.

"To have an ice cream on the way home !" said Penrose, hopefully.

"Not to wander too far away !" said Pixie.

"Well done !" said Daddy.

"Well remembered !" said Mummy.

With that they were all treated to the biggest, most delicious, Cornish ice creams ever !

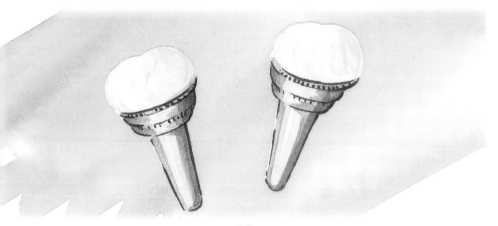

Here are seven words from the story in Cornish. Do you think you can learn them?

Kernow . . . Cornwall

Mammik . . . Mummy

Tasik. . . . . . . Daddy

Ebrenn . . . . Sky

Mor. . . . . Sea

Treth. . . . . . . Beach

Pell . . . . Far

WELL DONE!

Cut out
and
Keep
Book-mark

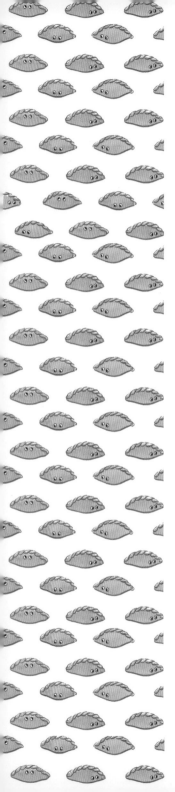

23